BRAVE MARTHA
AND
THE DRAGON

‹ SUSAN L. ROTH ›

DIAL BOOKS FOR YOUNG READERS
New York

FOR ALISA, WITH LOVE

Many people in France and America helped me with this book,
and I would like to thank them here:
Mayor Therèse Aillard of Tarascon and her office; M. and Mme. Chay,
Claude and Pierre Freychet, Lauro Garcia, Pierre Groshans, Valerie Jourcin,
Cindy Kane, Jean-Yves Martin, Régine Pascal, Karen Kolle Pickett, Louis Reynard,
Alisa Roth, Yvette Souliers, Marcel Valette, Père Bernard Wauquier, and the staffs
of the Loyola College Library and the Tourist Bureau of Tarascon.

Published by Dial Books for Young Readers
A Division of Penguin Books USA Inc.
375 Hudson Street · New York, New York 10014

Copyright © 1996 by Susan L. Roth
All rights reserved
Designed by Ann Finnell
Printed in Hong Kong
First Edition
1 3 5 7 9 10 8 6 4 2

Library of Congress Cataloging in Publication Data
Roth, Susan L.
Brave Martha and the dragon / Susan L. Roth.—1st ed.
p.   cm.
Summary: A young girl captures the dragon that has been terrorizing
the villagers of Tarascon. Based on a Provençal legend.
ISBN 0-8037-1852-7.—ISBN 0-8037-1853-5 (library)
1. Martha, Saint—Legends. [1. Martha, Saint—Legends.
2. Dragons—Folklore. 3. Folklore—France.] I. Title.
PZ8.1.R73Mar   1996   [398.2′09440454]—dc20   94-41631   CIP   AC

The collages for this book consist of cut paper and fabric. Most of the fabrics
are Provençal prints, characterized by bright, flowery patterns.

*A*long the banks of the Rhône River in the gentle hills of Provence, there is an ancient little village called Tarascon. The people there were always very happy…

In the morning Monsieur Claude's sheep were gone, without leaving even a bit of wool behind. The townspeople ran to the bell tower and called to Farmer Pierre: "What did you see? Who took our animals?" But Farmer Pierre was fast asleep.

"A fine watchman you are!" said Martin the innkeeper. "Tonight *I* shall take the watch."

He had three cups of strong coffee after supper and was wide awake all night until just before dawn. Then his head bobbed down to his chest. Suddenly there was a terrible roar.

The innkeeper sat up with a start and peered into the darkness. Something long and green and studded with sharp red spikes was rushing past the church. But when he rubbed his eyes to see better, nothing was there.

The sun shone yellow over the river as the townspeople ran to the bell tower. Madame Pascal was sobbing. Her cow was nowhere to be seen.

"I think I saw a piece of a monster in the night," the innkeeper said. "It made an unholy racket, and its tail was long and green and covered with sharp red spikes. I had one good look, but in a blink it was gone."

"Oh, oh, ohhhhh!" moaned the crowd.

"*I* shall take the watch," said the mayor.

The mayor sat in a chair on the balcony of town hall all that night. He was so worried for his people that he could not have slept even if he had wanted to.

Shortly before daybreak there was a terrible roar. The mayor crouched down and peeked through the railing.

On the street below ran a fiery dragon with smoldering eyes and smoke puffing from his nostrils. He had wild black hair on his giant head, and his huge green body bristled with sharp red spikes. He had six fat legs and six fat feet, and each fat foot had six long claws. His dreadful green tail ended in a knot. The mayor fainted flat on the balcony floor.

The next morning his wife poured icy water on his face to revive him. The mayor sat up and told everyone what he had seen and heard.

"My dogs are missing!" yelled Marcel the butcher from the crowd.

"Oh, no!" breathed the people.

The mayor stood tall on the balcony. "My friends, these are terrible times. We must bring the rest of our animals into our houses tonight. Every sheep, every goat, every pig, goose, dog, and cat. Lock your windows, bolt your doors. There is nothing else we can do. Be strong, my friends," the mayor said.

That day business was very good for the locksmith of the village. And that night the houses were very crowded.

Nobody slept well except the mayor. Once again he decided to sit up on the balcony, but by midnight his head was nodding. As the soft wind blew in the yellow Provençal morning, and the townspeople slowly gathered, he pinched himself awake and dutifully took charge.

The villagers had just accounted for all the animals when Madame Galette, the baker's wife, ran wailing into their midst.

"My boy! Naughty Bernard! He's not here! Yesterday the baker bolted both the doors and locked all the windows, but the front door was open this morning, and Naughty Bernard is GONE!"

"EEEEEEEEE!" cried all the mothers.

"OOOOOOOOO!" cried all the fathers.

"Here I am," cried a very frightened Naughty Bernard from the top of the chestnut tree in front of town hall. Naughty Bernard climbed down to the lowest branch and then slid to the ground. The seat of his pants had been ripped away. The baker's wife and Baker Galette himself pushed their way through the crowd and hugged him and kissed him.

"Naughty Bernard!" boomed the mayor. "Tell us exactly what happened!"

Naughty Bernard spoke in a shaking voice. "I didn't mean to be naughty. I thought I could save our town. All night I hid behind the posts under the town hall balcony. Just before dawn there was a terrible roar. And then I saw the fiery green dragon, covered with red spikes, just as the mayor has said."

"Yes!" said the mayor. "Go on."

"I hunched down," continued Naughty Bernard. "But the dragon saw me in the darkness with his burning eyes. He ran toward me on his six green legs. I started to run away, but he followed me. Closer and closer he came. He reached out his claws and caught my pants, but I didn't stop. I ran and ran, right up the chestnut tree. From the highest branches I watched him disappear into the river, and the water sizzled and steamed."

The whole town trembled. "What can we do?" they asked one another. "What can we do?"

At just this moment, everyone heard the sound of a clear, true voice. A young girl turned the corner, singing.

She was tall and thin and barefoot. She wore a simple dress tied with a long, silky sash. Her hair hung in dark curls, and her face was fresh and rosy. She spoke softly, and everyone hushed to listen.

"Good people, why do you look so frightened and sad on this sunlit day?"

The mayor told the girl all about the missing animals and the terrible green dragon with his sharp red spikes, smoldering eyes, six swift legs, and long, dreadful tail with the knot at the end. The young girl gazed up at the mayor.

"I should like to meet this dragon of yours," she said.

"Oh, I wouldn't advise that!" said the mayor quickly.

"Stay safe with us, mademoiselle," said the baker's wife. "I shall double bolt the doors tonight. What is your name?"

"Martha," said the girl. "You are kind to this poor traveler."

And so Martha went home with Baker Galette, his wife, and their son, Naughty Bernard, and she was made to feel very welcome.

That evening she was given a little bed in the spare room. "If you hear any strange noise at all, call at once for the baker," warned Madame Galette.

"Thank you, madame," said Martha quietly.

But in the stillness before dawn, when the fire had burned its last, Martha pushed back her quilts. Noiselessly she unlocked the window and stood on a chair. Without a sound she climbed over the ledge and dropped to the ground. She ran to town hall just as the dragon's dreadful green tail disappeared past the church. Martha raced after him.

"Stop!" she commanded in a voice that cut through the beast's terrible roar. The dragon turned his great ugly head. He billowed black smoke into Martha's unsmiling face.

"I am La Tarasque," he shouted. "I am the most terrible dragon in all of Provence. In my big belly right now are Farmer Pierre's goats, Martin the innkeeper's pigs, Madame DuPont's geese, Monsieur Claude's sheep, Madame Pascal's fat cow, Marcel the butcher's great big dogs, and the seat of a naughty boy's pants. And I still have room for a wisp of a young miss!"

Martha didn't move.

"Didn't you hear me?" bellowed La Tarasque. He opened his ferocious eyes so wide that smoke puffed out around the edges.

Martha looked directly into his fiery eyes with a steady gaze. "Shame on you for your wickedness," she said as she untied her long sash.

La Tarasque snorted fire and reared up on his hind legs. He lunged for Martha's head. But Martha made a loop in her sash and twirled it, catching one of the dragon's front legs. He stumbled, though he regained his balance.

"You will not terrorize this village!" said Martha, stamping her bare foot so hard that the cobblestones rattled.

La Tarasque surrounded her. Flames snapped from his eyeballs. Martha, with a flick of her wrist, flipped her sash again.

"I know the difference between good and evil," she said fiercely. "And you are going to know the difference too."

Now La Tarasque's two front feet were bound. He ran in a circle, around and around Martha, snatching at her furiously with his back claws. He scratched her thin arm and made six bloody stripes from her elbow to her wrist. Undaunted, Martha looped her sash once more and encircled the whole dragon. Dodging his snaky tail, she whipped her sash in the air again and again, catching his back legs with it, one after the other.

La Tarasque streaked the night sky with red lightning, and his thundering cry roiled the air.

"You shall not stay here," said Martha, cool as rain.

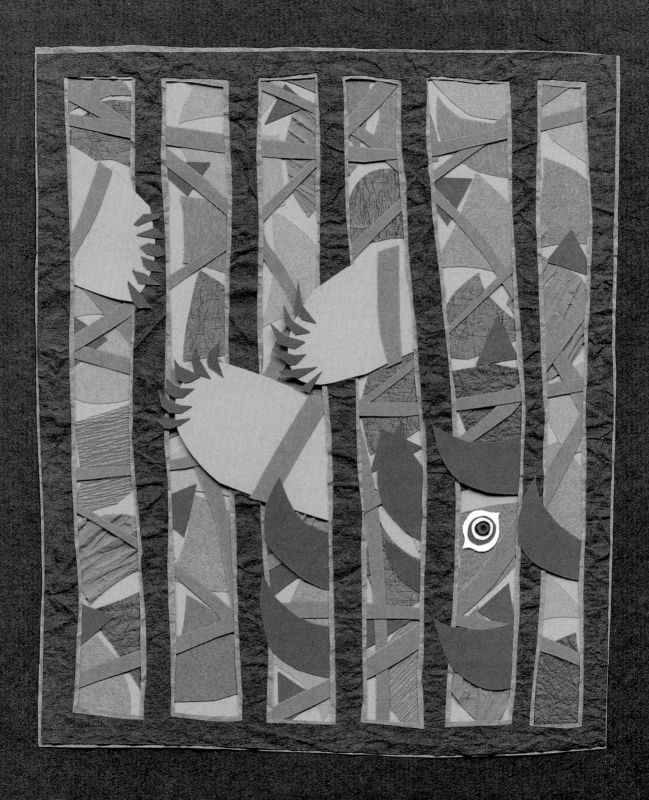

She tied a knot with the last of her sash and pulled the snarling, bawling, struggling dragon all the way to the dungeon, where she left him locked behind bars.

Just before the last star disappeared into morning, Martha arrived back at the baker's house. She climbed through the window, bound her scratched arm, bolted the window, and slipped into her little bed, sure that no one had seen her.

An hour later the people gathered again in front of town hall. Everything had gone well the night before. All the animals had been counted, all the children had awakened safe in their beds.

Martha stood in the street with Baker Galette, his wife, and Naughty Bernard. The mayor leaned over his railing. "I see that Naughty Bernard is safe. And you, mademoiselle—I hope you had a good night. But what is this? What happened to your poor arm?" Martha quickly pulled back her shawl, which had slipped and revealed her bandaged scratches.

"Whatever happened to you, Martha?" demanded Madame Galette.

"Just a scratch. Really, it's nothing," Martha said with a laugh. But the townspeople crowded around her, waiting for an explanation.

And then Naughty Bernard's piping voice was heard. All in one breath he said, "It's NOT NOTHING! Martha caught the dragon, she saved our village, I saw her do it, but he scratched her, she tied him up with her long silky sash, see, she's not wearing it! And she dragged him to the dungeon! She locked the dragon up! She ran back to our house and was in bed before morning!"

"No!" murmured the people in disbelief. Then someone tugged at Martha's bandage. Her six red ribbons of valor glistened in the sunlight.

"Oh, Martha!" shouted the people. "Hurrah for Martha!" shouted the people. "Brave Martha!" shouted the people. "Thank you, Martha!" shouted the people.

Martha was placed on a chair and lifted high in the air. The grandfathers tossed their caps and the grandmothers waved their handkerchiefs.

"I only wanted to help," said Martha.

"Just a minute, Naughty Bernard!" said his mother, loud and angry enough to be heard through the din. "How do YOU know this happened?"

"I was there watching," said Naughty Bernard, proudly at first. Then he looked at his mother and covered his mouth with both hands.

"Oh, you naughty Naughty Bernard!" barked Madame Galette. "You almost deserve to be tied up and dragged to the dungeon yourself! Didn't I tell you not to leave the house?"

Martha turned her cool eyes to the baker's wife. "I suppose you are right to feel angry, madame. But Bernard only went to protect me. If you forgive me, then please forgive him too."

"Since it ended so well, let's have no more scoldings today," said the mayor. "After all, the village is safe!"

And with just a little more sputtering, Madame Galette agreed.

*Martha's brave deed is still remembered in
Tarascon each year with a special festival called the
Fête de la Tarasque. There is feasting, music, and celebration,
and a fantastical dragon is paraded through the streets.
And the people say thank you to their beloved Martha
for saving Tarascon so long ago.*

The annual festival of La Tarasque, held in the Provençal town of Tarascon on the last Sunday of each June, dates to the late Middle Ages. This "fête" celebrates a miracle said to have been performed by Saint Martha.

In the New Testament, Martha was the sister of Mary and Lazarus. All were loved by Jesus. In the Gospel of Luke, though, Martha is rebuked by Jesus for worrying over housework rather than listening to His teachings as her sister does. In the Gospel of John, Martha witnesses Jesus's raising of Lazarus from the dead.

According to a Provençal legend, Martha, Mary, and Lazarus all sailed to France *circa* A.D. 40. Martha went to Tarascon, where she tamed the dragon that had climbed out of the Rhône River to terrorize the people and animals of the town. She sprinkled him with holy water and trapped him with her sash, then brought him to Arles to be killed.

The remains of the saint are said to have been discovered in Tarascon in medieval times. The legend of La Tarasque probably began then. The Church of Saint Martha, which houses her reliquary, was rebuilt in the 1100's to honor her.

When I visited Tarascon for the Fête de la Tarasque, I was quickly and warmly invited to take part in the entire five-day celebration. I rode through town in a Tarascon coach for one of the parades, I ran with La Tarasque in another parade, I stood near the priest and the mayor at the official blessing of La Tarasque, and I marched arm in arm with the town historian to the grand opening reception, to which the whole town was invited.

For all these activities many people wore traditional Provençal costumes (there are infinite varieties), or modern clothes made of Provençal cloth. The cotton fabrics, with bright patterns inspired by Indian paisley prints, are used in Provence for everything from curtains and upholstery to tablecloths, napkins, cushions, and of course, clothing. No two prints are the same.

The legend of La Tarasque contains a discrepancy that could puzzle a historian: It is the story of a first-century saint who saved a town in medieval times. For this reason and because of my intense visual impressions of modern Tarascon, I have chosen not to set the story in any particular era. For me it is a tale of sounds, tastes, smells, and millions of unmatched colorful patterns of cloth under dazzling yellow sunlight—all swirling around a great green dragon with bright red spikes.—S.L.R.